BTB 10°° 6/00

THE BEARS' VACATION

By Stan and Jan Berenstain

BEGINNER BOOKS   A Division of Random House, Inc.

This title was originally catalogued by the Library of Congress as follows: Berenstain, Stanley. The bears' vacation, by Stan and Jan Berenstain. [New York] Beginner Books [1968] 64 p. col. illus. 24 cm. "B-52" I. Berenstain, Janice, joint author. II. Title PZ8.3.B4493Be 68-28460 ISBN 0-394-80052-4 ISBN 0-394-90052-9 (lib. bdg.)

50 49 48 47 46

Hooray! Hooray!
We're on our way!
Our summer vacation
starts today!

And here we are.
What a wonderful trip!
Let's get in the water!
Let's go for a dip!

Small Bear! Small Bear!
Don't you go too far.
I want to see you
wherever you are.

8

Don't you worry.
Don't you fear.
I'll show him
all the dangers here.

I'm watching, Dad!
I'm all set to go!

Then here is the first rule
you should know.
Obey all warning signs!
Look around.
Are there any warning signs
to be found?

There is one.
And I think
you should know
it says in big letters,
STRONG UNDERTOW!

Ah, yes, Small Bear.
You're right! It does!
Do you see how good
my first rule was?

Yes, Papa! Here!
Catch hold of this line.

I'll be safe when I swim now.
That lesson was fine.

You will be safe
when diving, too,
after I give you
rule number two.

Look first. Then dive
when all is clear.
Now let's take a look.
Is there anything near?

Yes, Dad, there is.
I see a twig!

Never mind that!
It's not very big.

You proved it, Dad.
Even a twig
can be bad.

Right, my son.
That is very true.
It's a pleasure to teach
these rules to you.

Dad, I'll remember
the rules you gave.
Now let's go surfing.
Let's ride on a wave.

Now we go on
to rule number three.
Beware of all rocks
when surfing at sea.

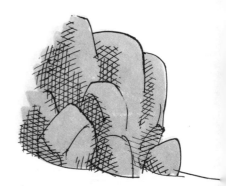

Look, Papa! Rocks!
Right there ahead!
We should beware of them
as you said.

Those rocks are much
too far away.
The surf will not
reach those rocks today.

Then, on the other hand,
we might
end up on those rocks.
You see? I was right!

I think I understand
safety now.
Thank you, Dad,
for showing me how!

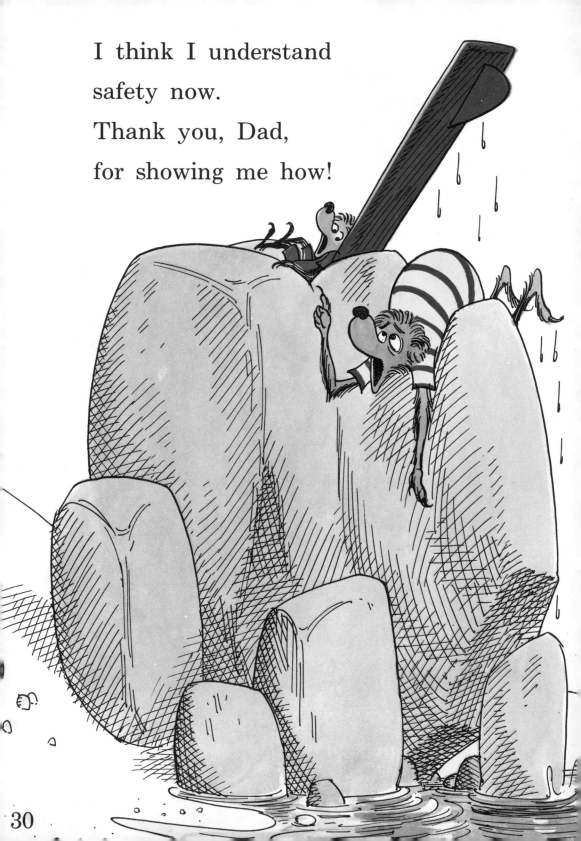

But I have much more
to tell you, my son.
My safety rules
have only begun!

When people vacation
at the shore,
they like to take walks.
They like to explore.

So watch your step
is rule number four.
There are many sharp shells
along the shore.

35

Here's a sharp one!
I'll step with care.
But may I keep it?
It looks quite rare.

Wait now! Don't touch
anything yet!
There's another rule
you have to get!

Here it is . . .
rule number five.
Watch what you touch.
It may be alive!

Rules four and five
are good to know.
Now I'll be safe
wherever I go.

Not quite, my son.
Hop into this boat!
You must learn the rule
for safety afloat!

Out in a boat,
you must take care.
And here is rule number six,
Small Bear.

Keep a sharp lookout!
It's easy to do.
Watch me, now!
I'll do it for you!

43

See? Like this!
Only a fool
would sail on the sea
without this rule!

It's a very good rule.
I can see that, Dad.
Without it, things might
get very bad!

I've been happy to learn
all you had to teach.
Are we ready, now,
to go back to the beach?

I have one rule more
before we go,
and then you'll know
all you need to know.

One more thing
people do at the shore. . .
they go underwater
and explore.

In exploring
underwater places,
there are many, many
dangerous spaces.

And my last rule
is simple and clear:
Stay out of caves
when exploring down here!

Hmmm. This cave
is big and wide!
It might be safe
to go inside.

But, Papa, do you
think you should?
Something tells me
it wouldn't be good!

As I was saying,
stay out of small spaces,
and any other
dangerous places!

WOW!
We learned that rule
very fast!

Tell me, Dad,

was that the last?

Yes, that rule
was the very last one.
My safe vacation rules
are done!

Ma!
You won't have to worry
any more!
Pa taught me how
to be safe at the shore!